All Because I'm Older

OTHER YEARLING BOOKS
YOU WILL ENJOY:

YEARLING BOOKS/YOUNG YEARLINGS/YEARLING CLASSICS are designed especially to entertain and enlighten young people. Patricia Reilly Giff, consultant to this series, received her bachelor's degree from Marymount College. She holds a master's degree in history from St. John's University, and a Professional Diploma in Reading from Hofstra University. She was a teacher and reading consultant for many years, and is the author of numerous books for young readers.

For a complete listing of all Yearling titles, write to
Dell Readers Service, P.O. Box 1045,
South Holland, IL 60473.

All Because I'm Older

Phyllis Reynolds Naylor

Illustrated by Leslie Morrill

A YOUNG YEARLING BOOK

Published by
Dell Publishing
a division of
Bantam Doubleday Dell Publishing Group, Inc.
666 Fifth Avenue
New York, New York 10103

ISBN: 0-440-40131-3

Printed in the United States of America

Reprinted by arrangement with Macmillan Publishing Co., on behalf of Atheneum Publishers

January 1989

10 9 8 7 6 5 4 3 2

W

For
Hannah,
Vaughan,
and
Nathan

All Because I'm Older

I don't know how he does it, but Peter always makes me do things I don't want to. He's only five, but he does it every time.

"Doggone it, John," says Dad, "you're three years older. You should know better."

I *do* know better, but it doesn't help.

Take last Friday. When we watch television, Peter sits in the blue bean-bag chair on the left and I sit in the red one on the right. Peter discovered that the beans were coming out of his chair, so he started throwing them one by one across the room at the wastebasket. I was trying to watch *Mork and Mindy*, see, and beans kept whizzing past my head.

Cut it out Peter," I said.

"I'm not even touching you," said Peter.

"They're going in front of my eyes."

"I'll throw higher," said Peter, and he did.

There wasn't any more zipping in front of my eyes, but there was a steady *plink, plank, plink* as they hit the wastebasket.

"Cut it *out!*" I said. "I can't hear."

"I'll throw softer," said Peter, and he started tossing underhand, but he's not so good at that, and a bean hit me right on the nose. I picked up a *National Geographic* to blast him one, but I missed and the magazine hit Dad's guitar instead. It sounded like an explosion in a symphony orchestra. And when the guitar fell over, it knocked down Peter's cocoa, too. I got sent to my room, and even with the door shut, I could hear the *plink, plank, plink.*

Then there was the time. Mom took us to buy sneakers, and while I was

3

picking out a white pair with green stripes, Peter was looking in the window of another store. When it was his turn to choose, he said he wanted a pair from next door. I went out to look at them while the salesman wrapped up mine.

The ones Peter wanted were real basketball shoes with black laces and gold writing on the sides. I wished I'd seen them first. I couldn't stand the thought of walking to school beside Peter if he had on a pair of those while I was wearing plain old white ones with green stripes.

"Hey, Peter," I said, "you don't want dumb shoes like that. All the kids would laugh."

"How come?" asked Peter.

"Look at the colors," I said. "Nobody walks around with gold writing on the sides."

"You sure?" asked Peter.

"Sure I'm sure. Think of everyone we know. Sammy Hofberg doesn't wear gold. Terry Kline doesn't wear gold. Chris Miller doesn't wear gold. They all wear white sneakers with stripes. I mean, they don't have to have *green* stripes, exactly, but gold writing and black laces . . . yuck."

"Well, okay, then, I'll get some like yours," said Peter, and we went back to Mom.

The salesman measured Peter's feet and went into the stockroom. A minute later he came out empty-handed and said he didn't have any in Peter's size.

"We'll go next door and get the other pair you wanted," said Mom.

"No!" Peter hollered. "I don't want shoes with gold writing on the sides. *Nobody* wears shoes with gold writing and black laces. John *said*. The kids will laugh."

Mom looked at me like I was really bad news. I don't know why I act that way around Peter.

Things are worst, though, where Stephanie, the baby of the family, is concerned.

Peter always tells me that Stephanie likes him better than me. And to prove it, he's always making her laugh. He barks like a dog and oinks like a pig and blubbers his lips at her, and Stephanie giggles.

The other night, Peter was feeding Stephanie strained pears, and she was laughing her head off. When I came out in the kitchen to make some peanut butter crackers, Peter oinked even louder just to show me how much Stephanie liked him. I stood behind him making my peanut butter crackers, pretending I wasn't noticing, but I was.

I realized suddenly that I had put peanut butter on both sides of the crackers, and I hit my head in disgust. Out of the corner of my eye, I saw Stephanie copying me. I put my hands over my ears. Stephanie giggled and put her hands over her ears. I shook my head back and forth. Stephanie laughed and shook her head back and forth. Peter kept staring at Stephanie, wondering what was going on. Then I picked up an empty cup off the counter and held it over my head. Stephanie picked up her cup of milk and turned it upside down over her head just as Dad came in the kitchen.

"John, what on earth!" he said, and Peter went out to play while I had to clean up everything, including Stephanie. See what I mean about Peter?

Sometimes, though, Peter makes me do a whole lot of things I don't want to do. Last Saturday, for example.

Mom said we absolutely had to have our rooms picked up by one o'clock.

"I bet I can clean up my floor faster than you can," said Peter, sticking his head in my room.

"I bet you can't," I said. That was my first mistake.

We tore around our rooms picking up T-shirts and sneakers and Matchbox cars and crayons, and I threw all my stuff on top of the bed to put away later, which I did. But Peter threw all his junk in his closet.

When Mom came up to inspect our rooms, she opened Peter's closet and said, "Hey, what's this?"

"I was having a race with John,"

said Peter, and Mom gave me a you-ought-to-know-better look.

Mom was trying to get the house ready for company, and every time she got one room straightened, Stephanie mucked it up again.

Dad asked what he could do to help, and Mom said he could do the shopping and take the kids with him, which was one way of saying *Why don't you all clear out?* But my mom's very polite.

Dad thought he was getting off easy because she didn't ask him to scrub the bathtub or anything and told us to put on our boots. I could tell that Peter was plotting how to get to the supermarket first so that he could step on the place that opens the door. That's how childish Peter is. Dad was trying to get Stephanie's feet in her boots, but they wouldn't go.

"See if she's still wearing her bunny slippers," Mom called from upstairs.

Dad pulled out Stephanie's feet. She was still wearing her bunny slippers. She was also eating a zwieback so she had to have a bib over her coat. I tied it for her, and Dad said, "Thank you," and I thought to myself, *So far, so good. No matter what Peter does, I'm staying cool.*

As soon as we stepped outside, though, Peter asked if he could take his helicopter to play with in the car.

13

And before I knew it, I heard myself saying, "If he gets to bring his helicopter, I get to bring my parachute."

"No helicopters and no parachutes," said Dad. "Get in."

Peter had done it again.

Stephanie sits in a special seat in the back, and Peter and I are supposed to sit on either side of her. The seat's not quite in the middle, though, and one space is smaller than the other. Peter, naturally, took the side that was bigger; and then he had to tell me about it, to make sure I noticed.

"I don't care," I said, just as cool as could be. "My window has more raindrops on it than yours." Did you ever hear anything so stupid?

"No, it doesn't!" said Peter, and he started counting. "Mine has eleven drops on it. Yours has bug splurps. You can't count bug splurps."

"Well, my window rolls down farther than yours," I said, making the whole thing worse.

"Huh-*uh*!" said Peter. "I can get my head way out, see?"

"Now, whose idea was that?" said Dad. "Put your heads back in."

I decided I wasn't going to let Peter get to me anymore and sat staring straight ahead.

Peter took out a sucker he'd been saving just to show off sometime when

I didn't have one. He unwrapped it very slowly, and each time he licked it, he held it out in front of him to see how much was left. He kept making loud smacking sounds to be sure I heard, and I wanted to plaster him, but I didn't.

A truck went by on my side of the car and Stephanie turned her head quickly to see it. And at that very moment Peter's sucker disappeared. I mean, one minute it was there, and the next minute it wasn't.

He started to yell like crazy. First he said that I took it, and then he said that Stephanie took it, and then we saw it stuck in Stephanie's hair. When she turned her head, I guess, she zapped it. I was dying to laugh.

17

My mouth just kept creeping up at the corners, and Peter went on bellowing about it to Dad.

"Well, get it out of her hair, for heaven's sake, and throw it away," said Dad.

Peter stopped howling. "Throw it out the window?" he asked. Mom had told us never, ever, to throw anything out the car windows.

"Out the window—anywhere," Dad said.

"Dad is a litterbug! Dad is a litterbug!" I sang. I was just trying to add a little humor, but nobody laughed.

Peter pulled the sucker out of Stephanie's hair, and she started to cry.

"See, Dad? Now you made her cry,"

he said, as he dropped it out the window.

Dad looked at us in the rearview mirror. He sure wasn't smiling. "I am trying my best to be patient. I am calmly driving this car so that we will all get to the store safely, and the least you can do is entertain your sister."

He was looking at me, but I wasn't the one who brought the sucker, so I just leaned back and folded my arms. Peter took Stephanie's hands and banged them together:

"Pat-a-cake, pat-a-cake, baker's man,
Bake me a chocolate fudge cake
with chocolate frosting,
Just as fast as you can.

"She's still crying, Dad."

The only supermarket that sells health foods is on the other side of town, so every week we have to drive for twenty minutes just to buy some special figs and nuts and cheese.

When we got there, Peter must have been feeling guilty about the sucker and Stephanie's hair and everything, because he tried to make up for it by unbuckling her seat belt.

Did I help him?

Did I wait so we could all walk over together?

What I did was get out my side of the car and run like mad so I could be the first one to step on the place that makes the door open. By the time Peter got there, he was yelling his head off, saying I got to do it first last time, which was a big fat lie. At least I think it was a lie. Well, maybe I did do it last time, but Peter usually beats me to it, so I don't know what he had to complain about.

But Dad just gave me a disgusted look, and we went inside.

Peter walked along the fruit counter, running his hand over the oranges and lemons.

"They've got cherries, Dad, with the sticks still on 'em! Can we have cherries, Dad?" Peter whined. "Can we? Can we have cherries, Dad?"

I didn't say a thing. I wanted Dad to know that there wouldn't be any whining from me.

Dad picked up a box of cherries and put them in the top of the cart.

"Hey, not there, Dad," I told him helpfully. "Stephanie will sit on them."

So Dad put the cherries in the bottom of the cart and Stephanie in the top.

While Dad was looking over the bananas, I sort of put my hands on the cart and began pushing it around to keep Stephanie quiet; and wouldn't you know, Peter was right there trying to push it too.

"Cut it out, Peter. I got it first," I said.

He grabbed hold of the side. "I'm guiding it," he said smugly.

"No, you're not. I am."

"Well, I'm guiding it better. See, you almost ran into that woman."

"Ha. I can steer this thing with my shoulder," I said, and proved it.

"Yeah? I can steer it with one knee!" said Peter.

And then there was Dad standing right ahead of us with the bananas, giving me that *act-your-age* look.

"John, go find a jar of olives," he said, and his voice was a bit raspy. "Peter, go get a package of bologna."

"Last one back is a rotten egg," said Peter.

I didn't say anything. It makes me sick the way Peter is always getting me in trouble.

I stayed away as long as I could. The only way to get along with Peter is to keep out of sight. But suddenly I heard him yelling, "She's bleeding! Stephanie's bleeding!" and I started running.

Stephanie was still sitting in the cart and she had pink stuff all over her face. There was a plum squeezed tightly in her fist. Dad mopped up the red juice with her bib and put the bib in his pocket.

"Sorry," he said to the produce man, who was frowning at us over the onions.

Dad moved us all into the dairy department and left us beside the Popsicles while he went off to look for butter. Peter was trying to open one of the boxes to see how many green ones were in it, so I had to

think of something fast. "You know what, Peter?" I said. "If you stuck your head in the ice cream case and counted to a hundred, you'd never get it out again. It would freeze to the cartons."

"Honest?"

"Yeah. That's what Sammy told me."

"Do it."

"Are you crazy?"

"Let's do it to Stephanie."

What a weirdo. "Mom wouldn't like it," I told him.

"Okay, I'll try it," said Peter, and he hung over the edge of the dairy case and put his head on the ice cream.

"You kids cut it out," said the

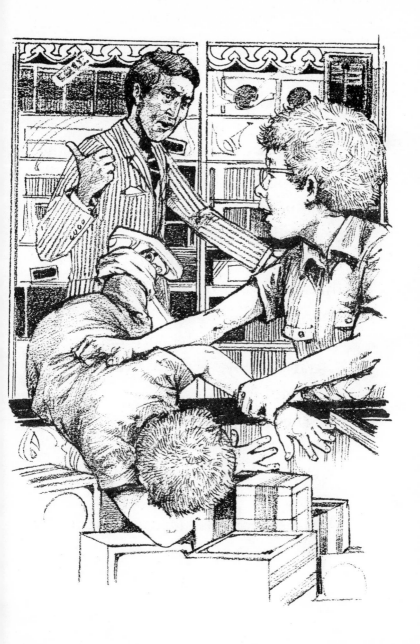

manager, walking by, and he made sure Dad heard him. As usual, I got the blame.

When we got to cereals, Dad looked more cheerful, like things were going to be better now that we were in the dry foods section.

"What kind of cereal do you want this week, boys?" he said. "Just one box."

"The one with the secret spinner," I said quickly. I really wanted that spinner.

"The one with the dinosaur," said Peter.

That's Peter. Anything to be different.

I could tell that Dad was about to

pick up the one with the dinosaur, so I said, "You'd better check it, Dad. Mom won't buy anything if sugar's the first ingredient."

Peter poked me with his arm.

Dad read the side panel. Sugar was the first ingredient. He put the box back and picked up the one with the secret spinner. He put that one back too, and ended up getting puffed rice, which tastes like paper.

Why didn't I keep my big mouth shut? See what Peter makes me do?

When we started for the seafood counter, Stephanie was trying to climb out of the cart, and Peter was trying to hold her down, and she was squealing at the top of her lungs.

I told Peter to bug off, and then I let Stephanie hold the bologna to shut her up.

Dad got in line to buy scallops, and Peter and I went over to look at the lobsters. They were sort of slimy and oozed around the bottom of the tank.

"See that one over there?" I said. "He's looking right at you."

"Blow at him," said Peter.

"He wouldn't like it."

"If I dropped a grape in there, do you think he'd eat it?"

"Better not," I told Peter. "The man's watching."

Dad just doesn't realize how many things I keep from *not* happening when Peter's around.

Suddenly there was a big *splat,* and water splashed all over the people who were waiting in line. Stephanie had thrown the bologna into the lobster tank.

Dad came over and got the bologna out. Stephanie was trying to stand up.

"Sit *down!*" he told her, and his voice was louder than Mom's.

Stephanie started to howl. Peter put his hands over his ears and laughed, and Stephanie, of course, howled even louder. A big lady in a floppy rain hat frowned at Dad.

Dad picked Stephanie up and stood her in the bottom of the cart with the groceries.

"*Please* push her around for a while until I get the scallops," he said, and his face looked a little bit purple.

"Sure," I told him. "Don't worry; we'll keep her quiet."

I let Peter do the pushing, and I walked along to make sure he didn't bump into the soda cans or something. We went around detergents and housewares, but when we turned the corner by the dog food, we went a little too fast and Stephanie sat down on the cherries. Peter decided he didn't want to push anymore, so of course I got the blame for the cherries.

Dad checked his list.

"Only three more things to get," he said. "You fellas stay right here and watch Stephanie. Whatever you do, don't let her climb out."

Stephanie picked up a can of lima beans and threw it over the side of the cart.

"Bad girl," I said, shaking my head.

She started to cry.

"Want a banana?" Peter said quickly.

Stephanie stopped crying and held out her hand, so I peeled one for her.

When Dad came back, there was banana all over the front of Stephanie's coat and she'd dropped the rest somewhere in the groceries. Peter was rummaging around looking for it, and I was trying to scrape off her coat with the edge of a cereal box. Dad was really mad this time. He didn't even care that it was Peter's idea in the first place.

He wheeled the cart to the front of the store and put Stephanie on the floor. His voice sounded high and crackly.

"Take her outside," he said, looking right at me, "and wait for me there. Don't let her run off; don't let her fall down; don't do one single, solitary thing to cause trouble."

I took Stephanie's hand and started for the door. Peter was walking along ahead of us, flipping all the levers on the gumball machines. Suddenly a big pink jawbreaker fell out and Stephanie dived for it. Before I could

stop her, the gumball was in her mouth.

"Dad! Stephanie's got a jawbreaker in her mouth!" Peter yelled excitedly. "She'll choke!"

Dad came over. He tried to make Stephanie open her mouth but she wouldn't. He pried one finger between her teeth and she bit it. He turned her upside down and the gumball fell out.

I didn't try to explain it to Dad because there was nothing to say. But I wanted to prove somehow that he could count on me. I wanted to show him that if it wasn't for Peter, everything would be great. I wanted to make the trip home so peaceful that he'd forget all about what happened when we were shopping.

I sat Stephanie on a bag of mulch and when she started to get restless, I stuck an empty grocery sack over her. When she started to cry, I made a little hole in the sack so she could see out. She stayed very still. Peter sat down on one side of her and I sat down on the other. People walked by and stared at her, and one woman said, "Well, what have we here?"

But Stephanie didn't move. I could hear her breathing under the sack. Peter was smiling, and I smiled back in spite of myself.

When Dad came out, he started to take the sack off Stephanie, but she

howled, so he put her in her car seat with the bag over her head. Only her boots were showing. Dad drove by the pickup place for our groceries, and then we headed home.

You'd be surprised how many things you can do with a kid sister in a sack. When Stephanie began to squirm, I would scratch my finger on my side of the sack, and Stephanie would jerk her head quickly to see me through the hole. Then Peter would scratch on the other side of the sack and she'd jerk her head to look at him. She was giggling.

"Now *that's* the kind of noise I happen to like," Dad said from the front seat.

Hey, look," said Peter after a while. "The gumball stuck to the bottom of Stephanie's boot."

Stephanie leaned over to look at it through the hole in the sack.

Peter found a matchstick on the floor of the car and stuck it to the gum. Leave it to Peter to do something weird like that.

So I found a piece of string and stuck it to the gum.

We looked all over the backseat and collected a paper straw, a feather, and a plastic fork from McDonald's and stuck them all to the gum on the bottom of Stephanie's boot. She held up her foot so she could see it through the hole in the sack.

There wasn't a howl or an argu-

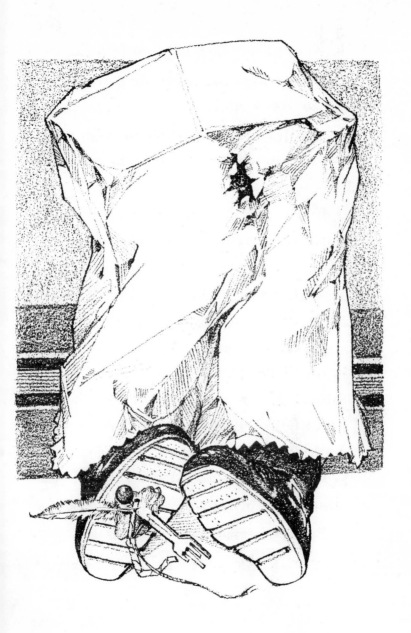

ment all the way home. There wasn't a lot of dumb talk about bug splurps, either. Dad didn't have to frown at us in the rearview mirror or tell us to put our heads back inside the car.

Ten minutes from home, he turned on the car radio. Five minutes from home, he began drumming his fingers on the steering wheel and whistling. And when he pulled up the drive and I offered to carry the bags in for him, he said, "I'd appreciate that, John."

Peter, of course, had to get in the act and offer to carry in groceries too, but I didn't start any stupid argument over who got to carry in the sack with the cherries or anything.

Where's Stephanie?" Mom said, coming out on the porch and looking around. "Where *is* she?" she repeated, and went down the steps to the car.

There sat a grocery sack with a hole in the middle, and sticking out from underneath were two boots. On the bottom of one was a gumball, a matchstick, a piece of string, a paper straw, a feather, and a plastic fork from McDonald's.

Mom took Stephanie out of the car seat and pulled off the sack.

"Boo," said Stephanie, and Mom hugged her.

Then she noticed Peter and me carrying in the last of the groceries, and she hugged us too. Dad came out to lock the car, and he was still whistling.

When we got in the house, Peter told Mom how I had put the grocery sack over Stephanie and made a hole in it and how quiet Stephanie had been and everything, like I was a genius or something. So of course, when he asked to play with my parachute later, I said yes. I don't know how he does it, but Peter always makes me do things I don't want to. He's only five, but he does it every time.